USE YOUR IMAGINATION

HOME ✻ SWEET ✻ HOME

By Kelly Oechsli

STECK-VAUGHN
C O M P A N Y
A Subsidiary of National Education Corporation

Up a muddy old road
on a big, tall hill
sat a rickety little farm.

First Steck-Vaughn Edition 1993
Published by Steck-Vaughn Company

Art Direction: Su Lund

1 2 3 4 5 6 7 8 9 W 97 96 95 94 93 92

ISBN 0-8114-8403-3

To that rickety little farm
and its tumbledown house
came a hard-working couple
and their faithful dog Sam.

What a terrible
what an awful
what a dreadful
mess they found.

Dusty floors
peeling walls
chairs that were
shaky and wobbly.
            CRASH!

Frazzled ropes, broken doors, pesky birds, frantic chickens.

So they all worked hard
and they all worked long
gathering the scattered straw
tending the frisky goats
sweeping the dusty house
milking the gentle cows.

And soon they were hungry
          they were starving
          they were famished.

So up the muddy old road to the tumbledown house
came the hungry farmer and his hungry dog Sam.

What a clean
what a tidy
what a well-scrubbed
place they found.

"Is there steaming hot soup and fresh-baked bread
and cheese to eat?" said the husband to his wife.

"No time for hot soup, no time for fresh bread
and your boots are muddy," said the hard-working wife.

"A farm's not a farm with dull knives and broken chairs."

"Well, a farmer's not a farmer
without muddy boots," the husband said.

But he ground the rusty knife
and he fixed the broken chairs
and they sliced their yellow cheese
and they had a simple meal.

Then because they were tired
    because they were weary
    because they were drooping
they all went to bed.

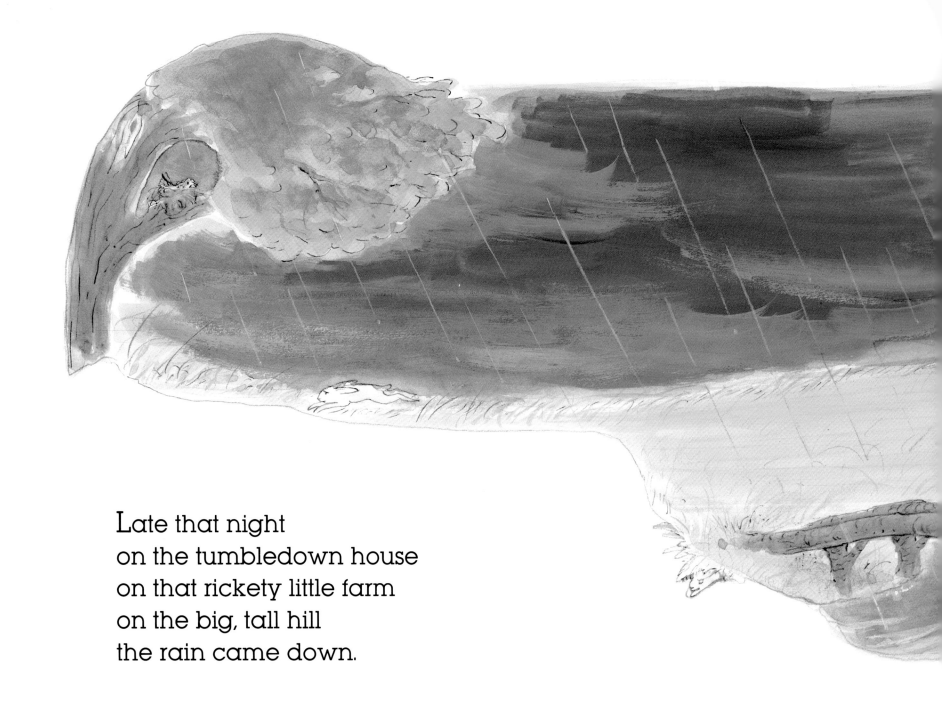

Late that night
on the tumbledown house
on that rickety little farm
on the big, tall hill
the rain came down.

That house was wet.
It was soaking
it was dripping!

"Oh dear," cried the couple,
"leaky roof
soggy mattress
wet pajamas.
This life is not for us!"

But faithful, wet Sam would not give up
and he ran very fast and he pushed very hard

till the neat straw bundles
were at the front door.

And he barked at the roof

and he barked at the road
till the hard-working couple
got the same idea.

They were excited
they were eager
they were determined
and they set right to work.

Now, up a new stone road
on a big, tall hill
sits a neat little house
with a fine straw roof
which a hard-working couple
and their faithful dog Sam
call their Home Sweet Home.

ADJECTIVES are words that describe or modify a person, place, thing, action, or quality. Colors and numbers are often used as adjectives: **black** cat, **blue** sky, **green** light, **seven** days, **ten** cents, **two** ideas.

Did you notice the adjectives in this book? See how these adjectives from the story describe or modify other words: **old** road, **hard-working** couple, **dull** knives, **new stone** road, they were **eager.** Can you find other examples in the story?

Adjectives—just one of many ways you can have fun with words.

Kelly Oechsli has illustrated over sixty books for children, including *Walter the Wolf, Germs Make Me Sick,* and *Peter Bull,* which was written by his wife Helen. His colorful and imaginative artwork has appeared on greeting cards and in all of the leading national magazines.

Born in Butte, Montana, Mr. Oechsli received his training at the Cornish School of Art in Seattle, Washington. He now lives in Hawthorne, New York.